BULLDOZER
Helps Out

BULLDOZER

Candace Fleming

Helps Out

and Eric Rohmann

SCHOLASTIC INC.

The construction site bustled.

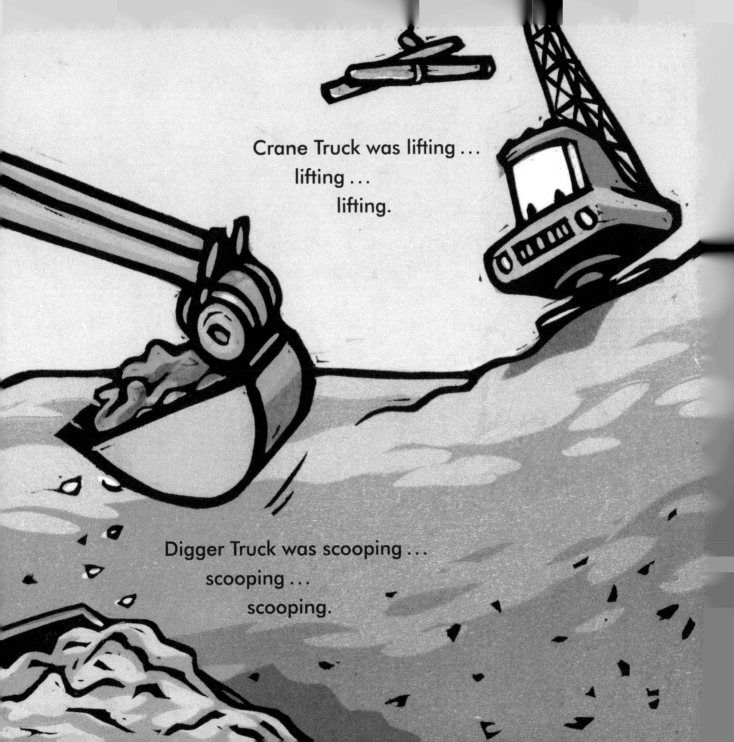

And Bulldozer was—
    "Watching...watching...watching,"
    he said with a sigh.

Puffing some smoke from his stack,
he bumped to where the other trucks worked.

"*I can help,*" he exclaimed.
He raised his blade hopefully.

The big trucks looked at one another.

"But maybe...," clanged Crane.

"Hooray!" squealed Bulldozer.
Honking his horn, he zoomed—*bump-vroom*—
to *his* work site.
Once there, he revved his motor.
He lowered his blade.

"Cha-

URRRRRRRRRRRT!

He sat, smoke puffing from his stack, for a moment.

Then he gave the pile
a little nudge.
Then a second.
Then a third.

And when he'd gotten it just right,
he hunkered down,
hushed and watchful.
His motor hummed,
soft as a lullaby.

Hours passed.

At last—
the other trucks bumped
to where Bulldozer was working.

He hadn't done a single thing they'd asked!

"I thought he was big enough," boomed Digger.
"I thought he was rough enough," rattled Scraper.
"I thought he was tough enough," clattered Grader.

"Move out of the way, kid," roared Roller.
"I'll fix that in no time flat."

But Bulldozer wouldn't budge.
Instead, he whispered, "Shhh!"

"How rude," belched Cement Mixer.

SHHH!

"Behave yourself," rattled Scraper.

SHHHH!

"You mind Roller Truck this minute," clanged Crane.

SHHHHH!

Then—

Above the banging...
rattling...
rumbling...
floated a tiny sweet sound.

The trucks quieted. And in the silence,
a chorus of gentle mews rose into the air.

"Is that what I think it is?" boomed Digger.

Bulldozer raised his blade.
He moved aside.

"They're pretty cute, kid," said Dump Truck.

"But taking care of babies?
Now *that's* a rough, tough job."

"I can do it! I can do it!" cried Bulldozer.

The big trucks looked at one another again.
"We believe you can," clanged Crane.

And he did.

For Caitlyn and Ann, noble foremen of our construction site
—C. F. and E. R.

ISBN 978-1-338-28087-6

12 11 10 9 8 7 6 5 4 3 2 1   18 19 20 21 22 23

Printed in the U.S.A.   40

First Scholastic printing, January 2018

Book design by Ann Bobco
The text for this book was set in Futura BT.
The illustrations for this book were made using relief (block) prints.
Three plates were used for each image. The first two plates were printed in multiple colors, using
a relief printmaking process called "reduction printing." The last plate was the "key" image, which
was printed in black over the color.